The Good Spy Guide

SECRET MESSAGES

Falcon Travis
Judy Hindley

D1562122

Colour Illustratio.
Colin King
Black-and-white Illustration:
John Jamieson

About this book

A Good Spy communicates with other members of his Spy Ring in special ways. They have a 'drop system' (a spy post-office) so that they can secretly pass messages even if they are watched by Enemy Spies. They have code books and secret plans and special code rings for sending signals in a crowded room.

That is what this book is all about. It shows you how to write code messages and disguise them, how to guard your secret systems, and how to set up traps and fool the Enemy.

There are instructions for making a miniature spy kit that holds everything you need for your spy messages. There are puzzles to test your skills and tips for practising code-breaking and secret teamwork. And there are instant codes, too—so that you and your Contacts can set up a Spy Ring and begin your work at once.

First published in 1978 by Usborne Publishing Ltd
20 Garrick Street, London WC2 9BJ, England

Published in Australia by Rigby Ltd
Adelaide, Sydney, Melbourne, Brisbane, Perth

Published in Canada by Hayes Publishing Ltd
Burlington, Ontario

The Good Spy Guide

SECRET MESSAGES

Contents

Passing Secret Messages

A Good Spy and his Contact know how to exchange messages secretly. They may need to pass on information about Enemy plans (this sort of message is usually written in secret code). Or they may need to arrange secret meetings or pass on warnings of dangers or emergencies.

Spy messages should not be exchanged openly. It is dangerous to meet your Contact often, or to be seen exchanging mysterious-looking papers. Remember that the Enemy may be watching.

This picture gallery is really a place where spies rendezvous (meet by arrangement).

They pretend they have come to see the pictures —hoping to put the Enemy off the scent.

If they think they are being watched, they can put their emergency plans into operation . . .

and secretly exchange their messages without even showing that they know each other.

Good Spies exchange messages so secretly that Enemy Spies never see them do it—and may not even suspect that they know each other. Below you can see some of the ways they work together.

If you set up a spy ring (a group of spies who work together) it is a good idea to work out several plans like this, and emergency signals for a quick change of plan. Later on there are hints on how to do this.

1 Letterbox Method

This spy never meets his Contact, but he often goes to the library that his Contact uses.

The librarian is really a letter box (someone who keeps messages for spies). She passes the message.

1 Using a Drop

This spy never meets his Contact. He leaves him messages at a spot they have agreed on.

In spy language this is called a 'drop'. Later his Contact visits the drop and collects the message.

5

Using Drops

It is important to have several drops in case one is spotted by an Enemy agent. You also need to choose another spot—called a signpost—where you can leave your Contact a signal to show which drop you have used. Each one should be out of sight of the others, so that the Enemy can not watch them all at once.

1. DROP 1.
(HIDDEN BY A BEND IN THE PATH).

FOLLOW THE SPY TO SEE HOW HE PLANS HIS ROUTE

4. SIGNPOST
(KNOTTED-STRING SIGNAL ON TWIG)

Choosing a Drop

Find a spot where you can be hidden from view for a short time, without looking suspicious. Look round the area carefully, watching how people come and go, and noticing what happens at different times of the day or week.

Approach your drop from all directions, to work out when and how a passerby might catch a glimpse of you. Will you see them coming? What action could you take to avoid them?

Then find a good hiding place there. See pages 22 and 23 for more ideas.

When leaving a message, plan your route so that if one drop looks risky you can easily go on to the others. Always walk slowly, stopping to look at the flowers or watch the birds, in case you are being followed. Then you will not look suspicious. Go to the signpost last, and leave a signal to show where the message is.

Using a Signpost

Decide with your contact on a few simple signals to leave at the signpost to tell him which drop you have used—perhaps a chalk mark or a coded matchstick. Pages 14-15 show lots of easy signals which the Enemy may never even notice.

Your contact should always remember to remove the signal at the signpost before he collects the message at the drop. To find out if he has got the message, you need not make the extra risky visit to your drop. Just walk past the signpost and see if your signal has gone.

Danger Park

Each of the spies shown here is about to leave a message at his drop (shown as a star). Some have chosen badly—and may be in danger. Would you have made the same mistakes? Try to spot the dangerous drops yourself—then turn the page to check the things you have noticed.

Danger Park Solution

These are the dangerous drops

A The spy is well-covered here—but so is anyone following him. There are so many turnings that it would be impossible for him to make sure that no one is near.

B The stretch of path in both directions means the spy can be seen from far away. If anyone is coming, he will have to wait a suspiciously long time before he is alone.

C To dodge away from the main path into one
& that leads nowhere will arose suspicion—
D particularly if you do it again and again.

E This spy can never know if he is being watched from the building opposite. Someone from the Enemy camp may be standing back from the window of an unlit room on the upper floor, following his every move.

These are the good drops

1 The spy can quickly check all the nearby paths, and the curved shrubbery covers him, even from a short distance away. If he has to wait for a while, he can pretend to be looking at the statue.

2 This spy also has good cover and he can easily check all approaches before he acts. The pond is a good excuse to hang about.

3 If the spy comes in from the main path (the one leading to the statue) and walks halfway round, he can check the whole area.

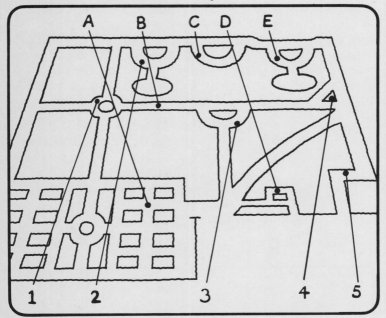

DANGEROUS DROPS

A B C D E

1 2 3 4 5

GOOD DROPS

4 Anywhere along the inside of this wall would make a good drop. From either end, the spy can see a long distance away—and he can hide quickly. But he should go from one end of the wall to the other, checking all approaches, before he takes action.

5 There is a good look-out point at each end of this stretch of path, too. From these points the spy can see anyone coming from a long way away. If the spy sees a passerby in the distance, he may have time to hide the message before he arrives.

Signpost Leaf Code

Your signpost need not be as secret as a drop. A Good Spy knows how to leave signals that hardly anyone will notice—and only his Contact will understand. The leaf code shown below is a good example. Just be sure to put the leaf in a spot where your Contact can see it but it will not blow away.

You and your Contact should each write down the signals and what they mean, as shown here. (This is your code book).

CODE BOOK

SFB—MESSAGE AT DROP 1

TEAR OFF A BIT OF LEAF TO LENGTHEN THE STALK

SFB (STALK THROUGH LEAF. FROM THE FRONT TO THE BACK) —MESSAGE AT DROP 1.

BACK VIEW

SBF (STALK THROUGH LEAF, BACK TO FRONT) —MESSAGE AT DROP 2.

TBS (TWIG-ENDS AT BACK, SIDEWAYS) —MESSAGE AT DROP 3.

TFS (TWIG-ENDS AT FRONT, SIDEWAYS) NO MESSAGE.

SPY TRICK

PRETEND TO BE IDLY FIDDLING WITH A LEAF—

SECRETLY MARK IT AND LEAVE IT IN A SPECIAL SPOT.

YOUR CONTACT PICKS IT UP TO FIND WHICH DROP YOU'VE USED.

LATER YOU CAN CHECK TO SEE IF IT'S GONE...

OR REPLACED BY A NEW SIGNAL.

COLLECT ANY SIGNAL LEFT BY YOUR CONTACT.

TSF (TWIG THROUGH STALK-LOOP AT FRONT) —MESSAGE NOT FOUND.

TSB (TWIG THROUGH STALK-LOOP AT BACK) —AVOID DROPS—MEET AT HIDE-OUT.

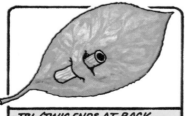

TBL (TWIG ENDS AT BACK, LENGTHWAYS) —AVOID DROPS —RETURN TOMORROW.

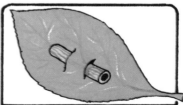

TFL (TWIG-ENDS AT FRONT, LENGTHWAYS) —LEAVE QUICKLY —WE ARE DISCOVERED.

Signpost Tactics

These spies are using several kinds of signpost signal. (The next pages show a code for each.) If you make chalk-marks, use a dull colour that will not attract attention. Put coded stones or matchsticks where they will not be disturbed. Remove your Contact's signals quickly and secretly, as shown.

RUB OUT CHALK MARK ON LEDGE

SHOE OF SPY USING GROUND-LEVEL TACTICS

THE ENDS OF THE MATCHES ARE A SIGNAL. PUSH THEM INTO THE GROUND

KNOTS IN THE STRING ARE A SIGNAL (COLLECT)

THE MARKS ON THE MATCHSTICK ARE A SIGNAL (COLLECT)

Ground-Level Tactics

If you have to bend over or kneel down to put a signal in place, or to pick one up—always try to think of a good reason for doing it.

For example, pretend one of your shoelaces has come undone and you need to tie it, or you need to pull up your socks.

Or start to limp a bit as you get near the signpost —then stop and pretend to take a pebble out of your shoe.

If you are carrying something, you could let it slip from your arms, or pretend it is so heavy that you have to put it down and rest.

14

Always behave casually while waiting for the right moment to use your signpost. With practice you will be able to use it even when you are under observation (being watched). Learn to memorize things like chalk signals at a glance— you can check their meaning in your code book later.

PRETEND TO TRAIL YOUR HAND ON RAILING WHILE YOU SLIP OFF CODE STRING

THIS CHALK MARK IS A SIGNAL— RUB IT OUT

MARKS ON STONE ARE A SIGNAL. (COLLECT)

Special Signpost Code

The meaning of each of these signpost codes is shown by just two signals—dots and dashes, long and short knots, or heads and tails of matchsticks. Choose whichever is easiest to use at your signpost. Both you and your Contact should write out the meanings and keep them in a secret note book like this.

Here are four different ways of making the dot-and-dash messages.

Use a black dot to show the head of a match and a circle for the tail. Write L for a long knot and S for a short knot.

1 MESSAGE AT DROP Q

2 MESSAGE AT DROP X

3 MESSAGE AT DROP Z

4 AVOID DROPS PLAN NO.1

5 AVOID DROPS PLAN NO.2

6 MESSAGE NOT FOUND

The dot-and-dash code can be used in lots of ways—chalked on a wall or a small stone, or even written on a matchstick laid on its side. Push the head-and-tail matchsticks into the earth in some protected spot—next to a wall, for instance. You can hang a knotted string message over a twig or some railings.

Making a Short Knot

Loop the string like this.
Then pull it tight.

Making a Long Knot

Loop the string like this.
Then pull it tight.

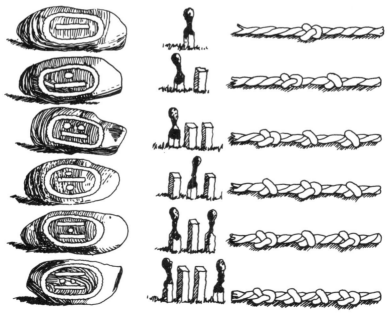

Quick Message Codes

Use these codes to make your messages secret. Each scrambles the letters in a special way. The code initials give your Contact a key.

Rev-Random

Write the message backwards (1). Then break it into new groups (2).

SPIES ON RADIO
1 OIDAR NO SEIPS
2 OI DAR NO SEIPS

Bi-Rev

Pair up the letters (1). Then write each pair backwards (2).

1 (SP)(IE)(S O)(N R)(AD)(IO)
2 (PS)(EI)(O S)(R N)(DA)(OI)

Rev-Groups

Group the message-letters differently (1). Write each group backwards (2).

1 SPI ESON RA DIO
2 IPS NOSE AR OID

Mid-Null

Break the message into even-numbered groups of letters (1). Split each group into halves (2). Put a dummy letter (a null) between the halves in each group (3).

1 SP IE SONRAD IO
2 S PI E SON RAD I O
3 SUP ICE SONDRAD IDO
↑ ↑ ↑ ↑

Sandwich

Write out the first half of the message, leaving spaces between letters (1). Write the second half in the spaces (2). Then group the letters differently (3).

1 S P I E S O
2 S(N)P(R)(A)E(D)S(I)O(O)
3 SNPRI AE DSIOO

Pendulum

Re-group the message letters (1). Mark a space for each. Write the first of each group in the middle space (2). Add the rest from left to right as shown (3).

1 SPIES ONRA DIO
2 _ S _ _ O _ D
3 PS
PSI
EPSI

If you receive a message and your Contact forgets to give you the key to the code, try these ways of finding which code he used.

OI DAR NO SEIPS

Start writing the message letters from the end and see if they begin to form into words.

PSEIO SR NDAOI

Try reversing the first few pairs of letters and see if you can join them into words.

IPS NOSE AR OID

Try reversing the letters in each group and look for words.

SUP ICE SONDRAD IDO

Cross out the middle letter in the first few groups. Try joining the rest of the letters into words.

SNPRI AE DSIOO

Starting with the first letter, write every other letter. Then add the letters in between.

EPSIS ANOR IDO

Write the middle letter of the first group. Add the first letter to the left, then the first to the right, then the second to the left, and so on. Can you see a word?

Who is the Traitor?

The four spies shown below are members of an international spy ring. One of them has betrayed their leader, who has been captured. Who is the traitor and who will be the new leader? Decode their messages (written in Quick Codes) to work out who they are. (Check your answers at the end of the book).

HOT TIP

You have discovered that the code names of the four spies are Owl, Elk, Bat and Fox. (Look for these letters to help you decode the messages more quickly). None of the spies (except the leader) is supposed to know which code names belong to the other spies. But both the traitor and the new leader have dropped enough clues for you to work out who they are.

CAIRO CALLING PARIS

IRF YOQUA REBBA
TOD OYPOU KEN
OOW WHOOF OXLIS

PARIS CALLING CAIRO

AMKLE WONKY
OFOHW SIX MAI
ABTON KLEROT

CAIRO CALLING HELSINKI

REH TIEN MAIKLE
ROTA BOT KLATS
UDEYAR TEBS AHX OF

HELSINKI CALLING CAIRO

WOW LLIB LO ERU ENL
WAEEDM RC YDON
EMAI EN STO WOQL

Hiding a Message

Here are some ideas for places to hide messages and ways to disguise them as leaves or twigs. Each arrow in the picture points to a hiding place. Good Spies are always on the look out for new places to hide their secret messages. If a bit of a message sticks out, rub it with earth to camouflage it.

Decide with your Contact exactly where your hiding place will be—make sure you choose one you will both be able to find again.

Hiding Places

1. Under the root of a tree or a bush.
2. In the cleft of a tree or a bush, or slipped into a crack in a wooden fence or gatepost.

3. Under a hedge or bush, disguised as a leaf or a twig, or rolled in earth-coloured plasticine.
4. Stuck under a bench.
5. Behind a plaque.

1 Preparing the Message

ROLL UP

TIE THREAD AND TRIM

Roll up the message tightly to make it less noticeable and easier for your Contact to get hold of. Tie it up with thread or a rubber band.

RUB ON DIRT TO CAMOUFLAGE

If you put the message in a very narrow place, leave about 1 cm of the thread sticking out. Your Contact can use this to pull it out.

Leaf Disguise

ROLL UP

STORE IN BOX

Roll a leaf round a pencil and tie it with thread until it is dry. Keep it in a matchbox until you need to use it.

Twig Disguise

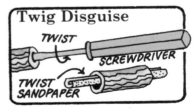

TWIST

SCREWDRIVER

TWIST SANDPAPER

6. Under creeping plants or lifted turf or moss.
7. Between the stones of the pedestal of a statue.
8. Under a loose paving stone or large rock.

Bore a hole through the soft centre of a short bit of garden cane. Then twist rolled-up sandpaper inside to finish hollowing it out.

Pocket Code Card

This code card folds up small enough to fit into a matchbox, but you can make 12 different codes with it. In each code, every letter or number of the message is swapped with another letter of the alphabet, or a different number. The pattern is below.

Special ways of folding the card show different alphabets. These are marked with key numbers on the edge. Be sure to tell your Contact which key number you used.

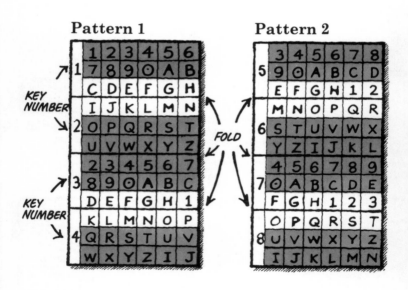

Pattern 1

KEY NUMBER

Pattern 2

FOLD

Use thin card or stiff paper, just the size shown here. Draw the lines and colour them. Copy the letters and numbers exactly like Pattern 1 on one side. Turn the card

over and upside-down. Now copy Pattern 2 on it. Use three different colours. Any will do but be sure to change the colour from row to row, as in the Patterns.

Folds to Use

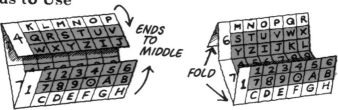

Fold in half to see codes 1-2, 3-4. Fold the other way for 5-6, 7-8. The ends-to-middle fold shows codes 4-1, 2-3, 6-7 and 8-5.

Fold the top edge down and the bottom edge up for codes 2-5 and 6-1. Fold the other way for codes 4-7 and 8-3.

How it Works

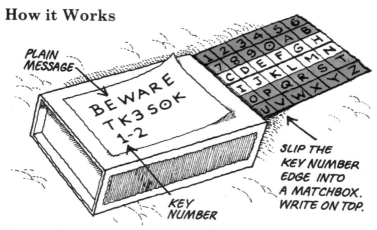

PLAIN MESSAGE

KEY NUMBER

SLIP THE KEY NUMBER EDGE INTO A MATCHBOX. WRITE ON TOP.

To encode a message, first print it out plain, like this. (A message not in code is called 'plain' or 'clear'.) Choose your key number. Under each letter of the message, print the letter or number in the same column in the same colour, moving either up or down.

For example, in the 1-2 code, shown here, the code letter for B is T and the code letter for E is K. To decode a message, fold the card to show the key numbers. Then, under each code letter, or number, print the letter in the same colour in the same column.

25

Code Breaking Practice

Good Spies test their skill and keep in practice
by exchanging coded messages. Experienced
code-breakers use complicated codes and make
their messages as difficult to break as possible.
New code-breakers start with easier codes and
may even give each other hints and clues.

To begin with, try some simple substitution
codes. These are codes in which the message
letters are swapped with the letters of a specially
scrambled alphabet—like those on the
code-card on page 24; or the keyword alphabets
on page 58. To help your partner you can put in
a clue, like the name of a month, a day of the
week, or a compass point.

Try decoding this message to see how it works.
It is written in an alphabet on the code-card.
The second word is a number from one to ten.

2R0 2RH00 80A 707X0H1 EP E9H 1FC H38Q A366
7002 91 W2 R0WZG9WH20H1 2E83QR2

Tips for Code-Breakers

When decoding a message, write it in large block
letters with plenty of space below each line. As
soon as you find the plain-letter meaning of a
code-letter, write it under the code-letter all
through the message.

Try to find vowels (AEIOU and Y), because every
word has at least one. Look for one-letter words,
which must be A or I or (very occasionally) O.
Double-letters might be OO or EE (the
commonest double-vowels).

Another common pair of letters is TH. The commonest 3-letter group (as a word or as part of a word) is THE.

Notice that punctuation marks help the code-breaker, so do not use them in coded spy messages. For example, the words OR, AND and BUT often come after commas, while THAT, WHO and WHICH often come before. Often a sentence that ends with a question-mark begins with W.

Try to look at words with a code-breaker's eye. Note patterns of double and repeated letters— as in tomORROw, LEvEL, lETTEr and CHurCH. Doing crosswords and playing word-games like Scrabble is good practice.

Code-Breaking Contests (for three or more people)

One person (the challenger) secretly encodes a message. The others try to break the code.

The challenger uses a code made with a secret keyword (page 58 shows how to do this). He writes down the plain message with the code-letters below it. Then he calls out the code-letters of each word for the others to write down. Each message should be at least 15 words long, with the code-letters in the same groups as the plain words.

Each code-breaker starts with ten points. He can secretly ask the challenger the meaning of any word, but loses a point each time. The person who works out the whole message while losing the fewest points is the winner.

Check Your Security—1

A successful Spy Ring must check that their security is good. If you suspect you are being watched when you are in your drop area to deliver or collect a message, here are some ways to find out.

If you know you are being followed, then you must find out if a suspect is really a member of an Enemy spy ring. The trick is to make Enemy Spies give themselves away and keep them guessing about your drops.

1 Are You Watched?

Never look directly at a suspect unless you are sure he is not looking at you, or cannot see you.

2

Pretend you are not interested in him, or have not even noticed that he is there at all.

3

A suspect may watch you only because he has seen you watching him. If so, get out of sight and show no more interest in him.

4

If the suspect is watching you, make it obvious that you are watching him. He will probably disappear and be more careful.

1 Checking a Suspect

Choose a false drop away from true drops, which you can watch without being seen. Hide nothing here.

2

Get the suspect to follow you. Look as suspicious as you can, without giving yourself away.

3

When you are sure you are being followed, lead the suspect to the false drop in a roundabout way.

4

Go to the drop but do not let the suspect see if you are delivering or collecting a message.

5

When you have left, the suspect will check the drop. As it is empty, he will think you were collecting a message.

6

The suspect has now given himself away. He will watch the false drop for a delivery and you can just disappear from the scene.

Check Your Security—2

If Enemy agents have discovered your drops, they will read the messages and put them back. They will copy the coded messages and try to break the codes. This is called interception. Because they replace the messages, you will not know that they have been read unless you check. Here are some ways to find out if your messages are being intercepted.

1 Paper or Thread Test

Fold up the message, ready for hiding. Open it out and put two tiny bits of white paper or thread in the first crease. Fold it again and put more paper or thread in the second crease. Finish folding the message. When checking, open the paper to see if the bits are still there. If not, they dropped out when opened by an interceptor.

Glue Test

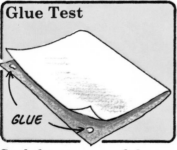

GLUE

Seal the corners of the first fold with tiny dots of glue. Then fold up the message. The seals break easily when the paper is opened. Check messages for broken seals.

Jam Test

WIPE JAM UNTIL THIN ENOUGH NOT TO SHOW

Fold up a message and open it out. Smear jam very thinly on one half of the back of the paper. Any fingerprints will show up on the jam. Do not touch it with your own fingers.

Broken Codes

You know that messages are being read by the Enemy. But have they broken your codes? Here is a way to find out.

Spoof Code

Write a message in a broken code, saying that all future messages will be hidden at a new drop. Say where the drop is, and what code will be used. Give it a name. Then write a message in a jumble of letters that look like a code. This is called a Spoof Code.

Spoof Drop

Hide the paper at the new drop—called the Spoof Drop. Use one of the message checks. Be very careful not to be seen at the Spoof Drop or you will not know if the message in the broken code sent the Enemy Spy there. Check the Spoof Drop for interception.

Fooling the Enemy

You now know that your codes are being broken and your secret drops intercepted. This is how to fool the Enemy Spies. Find a new drop. Change the codes to different ones. New drops should be out of sight of the intercepted one.

To keep the Enemy agents from suspecting you have changed your drops, leave messages in a Spoof Code at the old drops. Get different Couriers to deliver and collect messages as usual, leaving plenty of time for them to be intercepted.

Vanishing Secrets

Here is a good way to keep secret routes marked on a sketch map. Or you can use it for a map of your secret drops, places to meet Contacts, or even spots where Enemy agents are thought to be operating. The marks are invisible but you can make them appear whenever you need to check the map.

You can also use these vanishing marks for keeping secret notes, such as the code names of Contacts or their telephone numbers.

Draw a map in pencil of the area you want to mark. Put in landmarks, such as a school or park.

Wet the map all over with cold water. Lay it down flat on a newspaper. Put clean paper on top.

Draw in the route or drops with a pencil, pressing hard. When the map dries the marks will vanish.

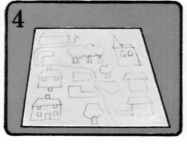

Wet the map again and the secret routes or marks will appear. Dry the map to make them disappear.

Spy Test

You have been captured and imprisoned by the
Enemy. The situation seems nearly hopeless.
You have no weapons nor spy equipment—only
what is shown in the picture below. Your captors
have allowed you to write one letter, but you
know it must not look at all suspicious. Not even
the cleverest code will fool them. How can you
use this letter to send a message to your Spy
Ring asking for help? Turn the page and see . . .

Invisible Inks

Your captors do not know that 'Mother' is the code name of your spy chief—and that you have all you need to write an invisible message between the lines of your letter. In fact, you have three methods to choose from. Read on and see see. . . .

Matchstick Pen

Sharpen the end of a matchstick by rubbing it on a rough stone. (If you are not in prison, sandpaper works better).

Spit Method

WRITE BETWEEN THE LINES OF A LETTER, OR ON THE BACK LIKE THIS

Wet the matchstick with spit and write lightly, as shown. Hold the paper to the light to check what you have written.

Juice Method

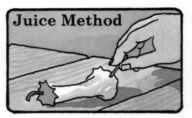

Poke the fleshy bit of the apple core with the matchstick to collect some juice. Write with the juice.

1 Wax Method

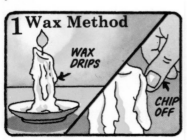

WAX DRIPS

CHIP OFF

Carefully chip away some of the candle drips. Try to break off some long, thin pieces.

2

HOLD IN ONE HAND

ROLL WITH OTHER HAND

Use the heat of your hands to warm the wax. Roll the bits into a pencil shape. Write with it.

1 Letter Signals

The initials used in the address of the letter are a signal to 'Mother' that the letter contains an urgent secret message.

2

Clues in the letter tell 'Mother' how to develop it. The next pages show how to plant these clues (called 'indicators').

Spit Developing

To see the spit message, the spy chief brushes the paper with watery ink. The message shows up as a slightly darker colour.

Wax Developing

GIVE A GENTLE SHAKE

To see the wax message, he sprinkles the paper with chalk dust, then shakes it off. The chalk sticks only to the wax.

Juice Developing

COOKED JUICE BECOMES LIGHT BROWN

To see the juice message, he heats it in a cool oven (about 250° F, Gas Mark 2) so that the juice 'cooks' and darkens.

Action!

Now that he knows where you are and the plan of the building where you are imprisoned, he can organise your escape.

Secret Indicators

Letters to other members of your Good Spy Ring should contain special clues to show them what to expect. Here is a good system to use—make sure everyone knows what the clues mean.

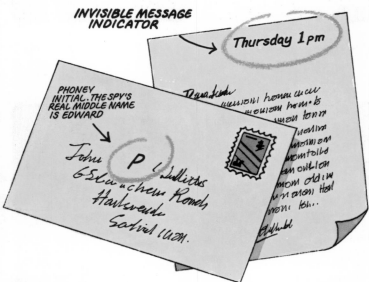

INVISIBLE MESSAGE INDICATOR

Thursday 1pm

PHONEY INITIAL. THE SPY'S REAL MIDDLE NAME IS EDWARD

Phoney Initial

Use this clue on the envelope, to show that it is a spy message and should be handled carefully. It works like this:

1 Phoney initial after first name means 'invisible message inside'.
2 Phoney initial before first name means 'code message—open secretly'.

Invisible Message Indicator

Agree on a certain day of the week to stand for each of the developers (powder, heat and wash). Use a certain time to stand for each of the places where a message might be written, such as:

1 pm—Along sides
2 pm—Between lines
3 pm—Back of letter
4 pm—Inside envelope

Testing for Secret Writing

Take care when testing an intercepted message, or one without an indicator. First hold the paper at an angle to the light, as shown, to check for any tell-tale glints. Then make your tests in the order shown on the chart.

ORDER OF TESTS
1. USE POWDER TO TEST FOR WAX MESSAGE.
2. USE HEAT TO TEST FOR MILK OR JUICE MESSAGE.
3. USE WASH TO TEST FOR MESSAGE WRITTEN WITH WATER.

POWDER

WASH

HEAT

Have all your materials ready so you can quickly run through the tests. For the powder you can use chalk scrapings, powdered coffee, dry mustard, red pepper or even fine earth.

To make a wash, mix equal parts of water and ink (or water paint). For a heat developer, you can use a light bulb instead of an oven. Hold the paper close, moving it so it does not scorch.

Secret Code Ring

This is an easy way to set up a secret communication link with your Contacts. Use the different coloured signs on the ring to pass messages without making Enemy agents suspicious.

Wear the ring with one or two of the signs showing on top of your finger when you want to pass a message. Try to look casual when you change the colours or move the ring from one finger to another.

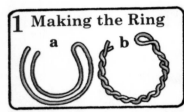

1 Making the Ring
a   b

Cut a piece of fuse wire long enough to make a double ring round your middle finger (a). Twist the two strands of wire tightly together (b).

2
c   d

Make four tiny tubes of rolled-up paper and colour each one (c). Slip them over one end of the wire and join up the ends of the ring (d).

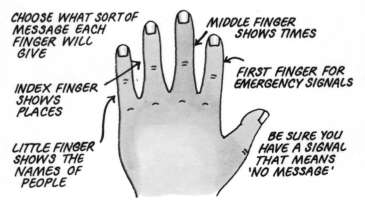

CHOOSE WHAT SORT OF MESSAGE EACH FINGER WILL GIVE

MIDDLE FINGER SHOWS TIMES

INDEX FINGER SHOWS PLACES

FIRST FINGER FOR EMERGENCY SIGNALS

LITTLE FINGER SHOWS THE NAMES OF PEOPLE

BE SURE YOU HAVE A SIGNAL THAT MEANS 'NO MESSAGE'

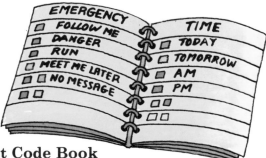

Secret Code Book

Keep a secret code book to remind you what the different colours on each finger mean. In case the Enemy finds your code book, you can put the words in code or initials just to remind you.

1 Enemy Alert

The Good Spy is waiting for a secret meeting with her Contact when an Enemy Spy arrives

2

Now the Contact approaches. How can the Good Spy stop him from revealing his identity?

3

The Good Spy moves the code ring to her first finger with red showing. This means DANGER.

4

The Contact sees the warning signal and walks straight on, unsuspected by the Enemy agent

Emergency Signals

Here are some more simple codes to help you pass secret messages to your Contacts. Keep a secret code book for these codes too, like the one on the previous page—then you will not forget what the different signs mean.

Make up your own order code to pass messages to a Contact at a conference or meeting without the Enemy knowing. Just arrange your pencils, pens, rubbers, ruler and other things in a different order along the top of your desk.

Face Code

DANGER　　　　**KEEP AWAY**　　　　**MEET ME LATER**

This simple face code is probably the easiest one of all to use in an emergency. Just sit with your first finger on, or pointing to, different

Pencil Code Set

To make this, you need an ordinary matchbox, three coloured pencils and a rubber band.

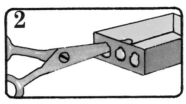

Make three holes, like this, in the end of the matchbox tray, big enough for the pencils.

Put the rubber band round the tray. This will stop it slipping. Push the tray into the box.

Arrange the pencils in a code order to pass a message. Put the set in your top pocket.

parts of your face to pass secret messages. Rest your head on your hand and sit still until your Contact notices that you are signalling.

41

Newspaper Messages

Newspapers, magazines and comics are very useful for passing secret messages. One with a message inside can be dropped almost anywhere without arousing suspicion. The message is so secret that only a Contact who has been tipped off will find it.

Use one of these two ways of writing the message and leave the newspaper, magazine or comic where people usually read them. You can drop it in a litter bin, leave it on the seat of a train or bus, or on the table in a cafe. But your Contact must be ready to pick it up or an Enemy agent or an innocent passerby may get there first.

Crossword Messages

Most newspapers and magazines have a crossword in them. Fill in the blank squares with the message. Write downwards only. Fill the other squares with any letters to complete the crossword. Leave the paper for your Contact to collect. No one bothers to look at a crossword that has been filled in. This is a way to pass an urgent message.

1 Pin-Hole Messages

On the front page of a newspaper is the date. Prick a small hole with a pin over one number of the date. This will tell your Contact which page you have marked with the secret message.

Turn to that page of the newspaper. Use the pin to prick holes over the letters as you spell out the message. Prick a hole in the space between the printed words to show the end of a message word.

To read the message, fold the newspaper so that the page with the message has no other pages behind it. Hold it up to the light. You can then see the pin holes and read the letters at the same time. Practice reading pin hole messages in secret. Then you will be able to read them while being watched but without arousing the suspicions of the person watching you.

Planning a Rendezvous

Members of a Good Spy Ring need many emergency plans for meeting at a secret Rendezvous and passing messages. These plans can have code names, such as RP (Rendezvous Plan) A, B or C. A Spy can then send a very short message to his Contact, just saying 'RP Q' or 'RP Y'. Then they meet at the Rendezvous, pretending they do not know each other, and pass a written message which is not in code.

Here are ways to pass messages under the eyes of a watchful Enemy.

Meet by a notice board. Stand near the Contact, pretending to make notes. Ask to borrow a pen from the 'stranger'.

Give back another pen, which looks the same. The message is hidden inside the barrel or rolled up in the cap.

Meet at a public building or tourist centre. Pretend not to know each other. The Contact has a map.

The Spy asks to borrow the map. He slides out the message hidden inside and gives back the map.

RP. N (Newspaper)

A Spy meets his Contact sitting on a park bench. They do not speak. The Spy reads his newspaper.

The Spy folds up his paper, puts it down and walks away. The Contact has to watch the Enemy.

She picks up the paper and reads it for a while. Then she leaves, carrying the newspaper.

Inside the newspaper is a long message. A bit of sticky tape on one corner stops it slipping out.

RP. B (Bag)

A Spy and her Contact carry bags, that look the same, with messages. They swop as they pass.

RP. H (Hat)

Two spies hang up their hats, with messages, in a cafe. When they go, they take each other's hats.

Secret Teamwork — 1

You can use these codes to pass information secretly to your Contacts when there are other people or Enemy agents near.

You can also use these codes to show your powers of thought-reading at a party. While you are out of the room, the others choose an object or a person or a number. When you come back you will be able to name it correctly. This is because your partner has used one of these codes to give you the information.

This and That

For this trick, leave the room while the others choose an object. Your partner puts it among some other objects set out in two groups (or lines). Secretly, you have agreed that one group is called 'This' and the other 'That'.

When you return, your partner points to these things one by one, asking 'Is it this one?' or 'Is it that one?' When he uses the word 'This' for things in the 'This' line or 'That' for things in the 'That' line, you answer 'No'.

But as soon as he uses the word 'This' for an object in a 'That' line, or 'That' for something in a 'This' line, you know it is the right one.

Name Code

Here is another trick that does not need any preparation—just an agreement between you and your partner.

Your audience will be baffled when you pick out a person or an object that they have chosen, without your partner even asking you any questions. You can just walk in and tell them which one it is. Or you could even let one of the audience ask you questions.

When you are out of the room, your partner arranges the audience in a line, or puts some things in a line. All the things can be the same—such as ten oranges—which will make the trick seem even more amazing.

Then the audience chooses one of them. When they are ready for you to come back in, your partner tells you secretly which is the chosen person or thing. He does this by the position of your name in the words he uses.

If he calls out 'Peter, you can come in now', your name is the first word. You know the chosen person or thing is in the first position. If he calls out 'We are ready now, Peter', the word 'Peter' is the fifth word. You know that the chosen person or object is in the fifth position.

To make the trick better, pretend you are getting secret messages from the different objects.

Secret Teamwork — 2

Secret Numbers

This trick uses an easy number code known only to you and your partner. With it, you can make your audience believe you can read a certain number in his mind.

When you are out of the room, he tells the audience to choose a number—for example 629. He then tells them he will say a list of numbers to you, but that when he comes to 629, you will know it is the chosen number.

When you come back into the room, but before he starts to say numbers to you, he decides when to say 629. If, for example, he decides to say it fifth, the trick is that the total of the numbers of the first one he says, add up to 5.

His first question might be 'Is it 32?' Your answer would be 'No'. But his question will have told you, without the audience understanding, that the chosen number is fifth— because 32 is made up of 3 and 2, which add up to 5. His first number could also have been 23 or 14 or 41, because the two numbers of each add up to 5 also. If he decides to say the chosen number seventh, then the total of the numbers of the first one must add up to 7.

It does not matter what the next three numbers he asks you are—because you know they are not the chosen one. It makes it more mysterious if he uses big numbers. For example, 32, 4619, 824, 99 and then 629.

THE SPOTS SHOW IMAGINARY POSITIONS

Pattern Codes

To do this trick, your partner lays out five cards or mats or books in a row. You have to guess which one they have chosen. The secret of the code is that each one has five imaginary positions on it, like this.

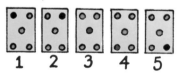

When you are out of the room, the audience picks one of them. Then when you come back, your partner points to any one of them and says 'Is it this one?'. Your answer will be 'No' but the position where he touches it will tell you which the chosen card or mat or book is. So if he touches it in the middle, it means the chosen one is third; or if he touches it in the bottom right hand corner, it means the chosen one is fifth in the row.

You can also do this trick with nine positions.

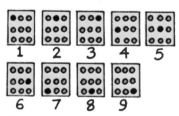

Then you can use nine objects in a row.

The code can also be used for passing secret messages. For example, you could hold your thumb on position three when you hand a book to a Contact, or you could scratch a certain part of the back of your hand. This might mean 'Enemy alert—follow me when I leave.'

Morse Messages

Morse code is useful for flashing messages in the dark and tapping them out in daylight. Make two quick taps for a dot and four for a dash.

Flashed Messages

Flash messages with a torch. Some torches have a button to press as well as a switch.

Draw the curtains in a room with the light on. Flip the edge of a curtain to flash a message.

Draw back the curtains in a room with the light on. Cover the light with your hat to flash the code.

In a room with a roller blind, pull it half-way down for a dot and all the way for a dash.

Morse Code

A	● ▬	H	●●●●
B	▬●●●	I	●●
C	▬●▬●	J	●▬▬▬
D	▬●●	K	▬●▬
E	●	L	●▬●●
F	●●▬●	M	▬▬
G	▬▬●	N	▬●

Count one slowly for a flash dot and two slowly for a flash dash. Make sure your Contact knows when to watch or listen.

Tapped Messages

Tap on water pipes or radiators in a building.

Tap on walls with a pencil or something hard.

Tap on railings. Your Contact will have to put his ear against them.

Tap on the ground. Your Contact holds a stick, puts his hand on top and presses his ear to them.

O ▬ ▬ ▬	V ○○○ ▬
P ○ ▬ ▬ ○	W ○ ▬ ▬
Q ▬ ▬ ○ ▬	X ▬ ○○ ▬
R ○ ▬ ○	Y ▬ ○ ▬ ▬
S ○○○	Z ▬ ▬ ○○
T ▬	FULL STOP ○ ▬ ○ ▬ ○ ▬
U ○○ ▬	QUESTION MARK ○○ ▬ ▬ ○○

Pocket Spy Kit

Here is how to fit all your basic spy equipment into a matchbox. It holds an invisible writing kit, hollow twig disguise, code-card, and all you need for signpost signals. Make three mini-pens —a pencil for code messages, a bit of white crayon or candle for wax writing and chalk for signpost signals and wax developing. The next pages show how to make dividers and a lifting string for fast action in emergencies.

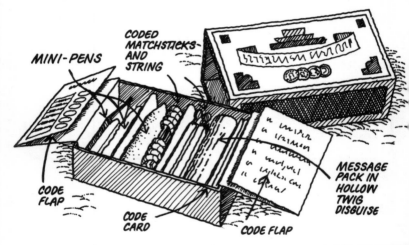

MINI-PENS

CODED MATCHSTICKS AND STRING

CODE FLAP

CODE CARD

CODE FLAP

MESSAGE PACK IN HOLLOW TWIG DISGUISE

For the container, you will need:
a matchbox
stiff paper or thin card (a postcard is good)
scissors and a pencil
strong glue and sticky tape
needle and thread for the lifter (shown on the next pages)

1 Code Flaps

LEAVE A TAB

MARK

CUT INSIDE THIS LINE

Draw round the matchbox on some card, leaving a bit extra. Cut out a strip slightly narrower than this. Do this twice.

Matchstick Holder

LEAVE A SPACE AS WIDE AS A MATCHSTICK

FOLD OVER

Lay six coded matchsticks (broken to size) on a bit of sticky tape, leaving a space in the middle. Fold the strip as shown.

String Holder

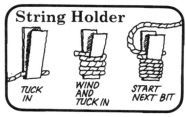

TUCK IN

WIND AND TUCK IN

START NEXT BIT

Tuck the end of the string into the fold of a strip of card, cut to size. Then wind it round and tuck in the other end.

Making Mini-Pens

PRESS HARD

ROLL PENCIL

To cut down a pencil, chalk or bit of candle, saw round with a knife to make a deep groove. Then you can break it here.

Message Pack

Cut strips of paper a bit narrower than the tray. Wind tightly round a matchstick, one by one. Tuck into the hollow twig.

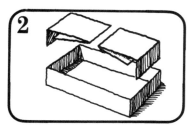

Fold the strips so that the folded flaps will fit together in the tray when you close the box. Bend down the tabs and trim.

WRITE ON THESE BITS

GLUE IN THE TABS

Write the codes on one flap and the meanings on the other. Then glue the tabs into the tray.

Quick-Action Lifter

Fix a secret thread inside your spy kit, as shown below. Then you can make the contents pop up instantly when you need them. Measure carefully—it will save you valuable time when you are in action.

You can disguise the kit to look like part of a stamp collection in case you are stopped and searched by the Enemy.

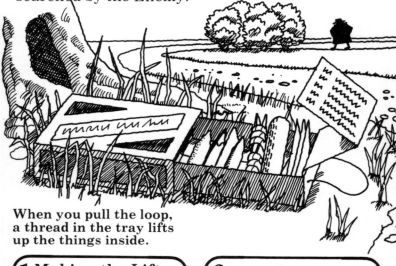

When you pull the loop, a thread in the tray lifts up the things inside.

1 Making the Lifter

MARK TWICE THE DEPTH

CUT OUT A BIT NARROWER

Measure and cut out three strips of thin card. Make each a bit narrower than the tray and about twice as long as it is deep.

2

LEAVE SOME SPACE ABOVE

FOLD AND CHECK

Fold each strip like this and check that it fits well into the tray. Dab glue inside and press tightly. Leave to dry.

54

Poke a threaded needle through the top of one strip. Knot it as shown. Glue this strip in the middle of the tray.

Now poke the thread through each end of the tray. Pull it just tight enough to lie flat in each compartment.

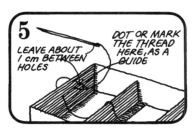

At each end, push the threaded needle back into the tray, like this. Make a mark on the thread where it comes out.

Make a knot in the thread just where the dot is. Cut off the rest. Pull the thread back in again and pack in your equipment.

Cut a piece of card a bit longer and narrower than the tray. Fold down the ends so that it fits just over the tray.

Glue a few old stamps to the card, making sure they overlap, like this. Staple or sew on one stamp to be the lifter.

55

Message Scrambler

You can use this sort of code for sending secret messages up to 24 letters long. You can choose any keyword and use one of the Routes explained below. If the Enemy Spies crack your code—just make up a new keyword and choose a different Route.

Keywords

Your Keyword can be any word in which none of the letters appear more than once. But it is easier to use words which have four, five or six letters, such as: ZEBRAS, WREN, GHOST, LAMB, SPIDER, SHADOW, BAKER or CAKE.

Routes

The Route is the direction in which you write out the words of your message underneath or beside your Keyword.

Here are some examples of different Routes—follow the letters of the alphabet to see how each one goes.

B R A Z I L
```
A B C D E F
G H I J K L
M N O P Q R
S T U V W X
```
(Side-to-side 1)

```
W | A E I M Q U
R | B F J N R V
E | C G K O S W
N | D H L P T X
```
(Up-and-down 1)

S P I D E R
```
A B C D E F
P Q R S T G
O X W V U H
N M L K J I
```
(Spiral 1)

Z E B R A S
```
A B C D E F
L K J I H G
M N O P Q R
X W V U T S
```
(Side-to-side 2)

```
L | A H I P Q X
A | B G J O R W
M | C F K N S V
B | D E L M T U
```
(Up-and-down 2)

S H A D O W
```
A P O N M L
B Q X W V K
C R S T U J
D E F G H I
```
(Spiral 2)

56

Sending a Message

When you want to send a message, first make sure that you and the person who will receive it, are using the same Keyword and the same Route.

So if the message you want to send is 'SPY ZERO SIX MUST ACT QUICKLY', and you decide to use Keyword BRAZIL and route SIDE TO SIDE 1—you set your message out like this:

B R A Z I L
S P Y Z E R
O S I X M U
S T A C T Q
U I C K L Y

Then, to put the message into code, you read off the new coded words in vertical lines, in the alphabetical order of the Keyword. So the letters under A of BRAZIL are the first coded word, and the letters under Z of BRAZIL are the last. Now your message in code reads YIAC SOSU EMTL RUQY PSTI ZXCK.

If there are not enough letters in the message you want to send, to fill the spaces under your Keyword—you must fill up the empty spaces with the letter X.

Receiving a Message

When you receive a message, you do exactly the opposite to the sender. For example, if you receive the following message—OTOQ LHNA CKTH CGIT GOTO OXIS, and you are using Keyword SHADOW and Route SPIRAL- 2, you first write down the Keyword—SHADOW. Then you write down the coded message like this: OTOQ, under the A of SHADOW, LHNA under the D, CKTH under the H,

CGIT under the O, GOTO under the S, and OXIS under the W. So now the coded message will look like this.

S H A D O W

G C O L C O
O K T H G X
T T O N I I
O H Q A T S

Then you simply read off the actual message by following Route SPIRAL- 2.

Keyword Alphabet Codes

You can make a good code by swapping each of
your message letters with the matching letter in
a keyword alphabet. Some examples are shown
below. Notice that each begins with a word or
phrase in which no letter is repeated. This is the
keyword. The rest of the alphabet follows.

If you find your own keyword, you can make a
code known only to your Good Spy Ring.

Plain Alphabets	Keyword Alphabets					
A	B	C	M	M	I	P
B	E	A	Y	I	M	U
C	W	R	O	S	P	R
D	A	E	L	F	O	C
E	T	F	D	O	R	H
F	C	U	A	R	T	A
G	H	L	U	T	A	S
H	F	S	N	U	N	I
I	U	P	T	N	C	N
J	L	Y	S	E	E	G
K	D	B	B	A	B	B
L	G	D	C	B	D	D
M	I	G	E	C	F	E
N	J	H	F	D	G	F
O	K	I	G	G	H	J
P	M	J	H	H	J	K
Q	N	K	I	J	K	L
R	O	M	J	K	L	M
S	P	N	K	L	Q	O
T	Q	O	P	P	S	Q
U	R	Q	Q	Q	U	T
V	S	T	R	V	V	V
W	V	V	V	W	W	W
X	X	W	W	X	X	X
Y	Y	X	X	Y	Y	Y
Z	Z	Z	Z	Z	Z	Z

Instant Codes—1

These instant codes are useful for sending written messages in code. In each one, a different shape stands for a letter of the alphabet.

On the next two pages are four instant codes. You can either learn them or use the pages for encoding and decoding your secret messages.. You can also copy them and change the order of the letters to make the code more secret. Give a copy to your Contact so he knows the code.

This looks very strange but it is easy to use. A line shape, or a shape and a dot, stands for each letter of the alphabet. Here is a message in code.

Semaphore is usually signalled with flags. Here you use the same positions of the flags but written like the hands of a clock.

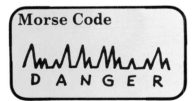

This is usually written as dots and dashes. Here tall peaks stand for dashes and short one for dots. A line means the end of a letter. A break in the line means the end of a word.

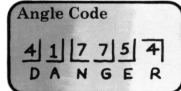

In this code, a line shape with a number written in it stands for the letters. Starting at the beginning of the alphabet, a shape is numbered 1 to 7. Then the shape is changed.

Instant Codes—2

PLAIN	PIG-PEN	MORSE	SEMAPHORE	ANGLE
A	⌐	∧	①	1
B	∪	∧ₘ	⊖	2
C	∟	∧∧ₘ	①	3
D	⊐	∧ₘ	①	4
E	▢	∧	①	5
F	⊏	∿∧	⊕	6
G	⌐	∧∧ₘ	①	7
H	⊓	∿∿	⊖	1
I	⌐	∿	⊘	2
J	⌐•	∿∧∧	⊕	3
K	•⌐	∧∧	①	4
L	∟•	∿∧	⊘	5
M	⊐•	∧	⊖	6

PLAIN	PIG-PEN	MORSE	SEMAPHORE	ANGLE
N	⊡	∧	◬	7
O	⊡	∧∧	◔	1
P	⊓	∧∧	◔	2
Q	⊓	∧∧	◔	3
R	⌐	∧∧	⊖	4
S	∨	∧∧	◔	5
T	>	∧	◔	6
U	<	∧∧	◔	7
V	∧	∧∧∧	◔	1
W	∨	∧∧	◔	2
X	>	∧∧	◔	3
Y	<	∧∧	⊖	4
Z	∧	∧∧	◔	5

Spy Language

Clear Message—A message not written in code.

Code-Breaking—When you work out the clear meaning of a code message without knowing beforehand what the code is, you have broken the code.

Contact—A member of your spy ring, usually one you meet by arrangement.

Courier—A member of a spy ring who carries and delivers secret messages, information or instructions to other members.

Decode—To work out the clear meaning of a code message using a key or indicator.

Developing—A way of making an invisible message appear.

Drop—A place where messages are left by spies for other spies.

Encode—You encode a message when you write it in code.

False Drop—A place where you pretend to leave and collect messages, or where you leave messages written in a Spoof Code, to fool the Enemy.

Indicator—An innocent-looking sign that shows where to find a message or how to decode it or develop it.

Interception—Getting hold of a message intended for the Enemy.

Key—A clue to the code used in a message, or the code itself.

Keyword—A word with all-different letters that is used to make a code.

Plain Message—A message not written in code.

Rendezvous—A meeting between two members of a spy ring.

Scrambled—A code that works by mixing up the letters of a message in a special way is called a scrambled code (or 'transposition' code).

Secret Agent or Agent—A member of a spy ring.

Security—Safety. When your messages and action are well-disguised or well-hidden they are 'secure'.

Signpost—The part of a drop system where signs are left to show which drop is being used.

Spoof Code—Letters jumbled up to look like a code to fool the Enemy.

Spy Ring—A group of spies who work together secretly.

Substitution Code—A code that works by swapping message letters with the letters of a scrambled alphabet or a symbol alphabet.

Wash—A mixture of water and ink or paint used to develop a wax or water message.

Answers

Answers to Who is the Traitor? Coded Messages on pages 20 and 21

These messages show that Owl is the new leader and Fox is the traitor. Have you identified Owl and Fox? Turn the page upside-down to see the answer.

Paris calling Delhi
(Rev-Group Code)
Our leader is caught. Owl is second in command. Are you Owl?

Delhi calling Paris
(Pendulum Code)
My code-name is not Owl. The traitor is Fox. Who is Fox?

Delhi calling Cairo
(Bi-Rev Code)
Fox is a traitor. Bat knows him. I am not Bat. Who is?

Cairo calling Delhi
(Sandwich Code)
Code names should be secret, but mine is neither Bat nor Fox.

Cairo calling Paris
(Mid-null Code)
If you are Bat, do you know who Fox is?

Paris calling Cairo
(Rev-Group Code)
Elk may know who Fox is. I am not Bat or Elk.
64

Cairo calling Helsinki
(Rev-Random Code)
Fox has betrayed us. Talk to Bat or Elk. I am neither.

Helsinki calling Cairo
(Bi-Rev Code)
Owl will be our new leader. My code-name is not Owl.

Identity of Traitor and New Leader on pages 20 and 21.

The agent in Cairo has let it slip that he is not Bat, Fox or Elk, so he must be Owl, the new leader. The agent in Paris cannot be Owl, and he has said he is not Bat or Elk, so he must be the traitor—Fox.

Answer to Code Breaking Practice on page 26.

The only 5-letter words between one and seven are three and ten. Did you guess that the first two words of the message are 'The three'? If so, you will have found that the message is encoded with the 8-5 key of the code card. It reads:

The three new members of our spy ring will meet us at headquarters tonight.